Honesty

A Level Three Reader

By Kathryn Kyle

The
Child's
World®

On the cover...
This boy is learning honesty from a police officer.

Published by The Child's World®, Inc.
PO Box 326
Chanhassen, MN 55317-0326
800-599-READ
www.childsworld.com

Special thanks to the Dunsing, Giroux, Matsuyama, Sanks, and Toral families, and to the staff and students of Alessandro Volta and Shoesmith Elementary Schools for their help and cooperation in preparing this book.

Photo Credits
© Bettmann/CORBIS: 25
© The Corcoran Gallery of Art/CORBIS: 22
© Joel Dexter/Unicorn Stock Photos: 3
© Romie Flanagan: cover, 5, 6, 9, 10, 13, 14, 17, 18, 21, 26

Project Coordination: Editorial Directions, Inc.
Photo Research: Alice K. Flanagan

Library of Congress Cataloging-in-Publication Data
Kyle, Kathryn.
Honesty / by Kathryn Kyle.
    p. cm. — (An Easy reader)
Includes index.
Summary: Easy-to-read scenarios, such as telling a store clerk that you
received too much change or telling your mother you fed your broccoli to
the dog, provide lessons in honesty.
ISBN 1-56766-089-4 (alk. paper)
1. Truthfulness and falsehood—Juvenile literature.
2. Honesty—Juvenile literature. [1. Honesty.] I. Title. II. Wonder books
(Chanhassen, Minn.)
BJ1421 .K95 2002
179'.9--dc21
                        2001007953

What is honesty? Honesty is telling the truth. It is important to be honest every day. Telling the truth helps us to get along with each other.

At home, you come into the house from the backyard. Your shoes are muddy. You leave a trail of mud in the hallway. Your mother wants to know who made the mess. Honesty is telling her that you made the mess.

At the store, you buy a candy bar. It costs 75 cents. You give the **clerk** one dollar for the candy bar. She gives you 50 cents back in change. It should only be 25 cents. Honesty is returning the money that does not belong to you.

It is time to do your homework. Your favorite show is on television. But your father said you have to finish your homework. Honesty is telling him that you are watching television instead of doing your homework.

At school, you find a jump rope on the playground. It is a new jump rope. You have always wanted one just like it. Honesty is giving it to your teacher instead of keeping it. Then your teacher can find the jump rope's owner.

11

Your brother leaves his candy on the counter. There are many pieces. Honesty is leaving it alone, even though you would like to eat some.

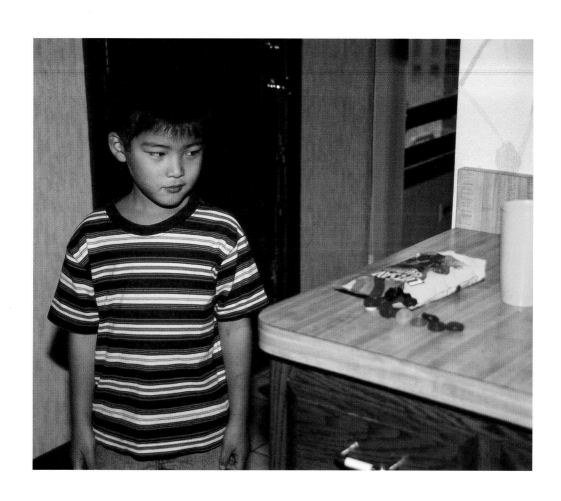

14

You had some homework to finish over the weekend. You forgot to do it. On Monday, your teacher asks you where it is. Honesty is telling her you forgot to do it, even though you could make up an **excuse**.

You are playing at a friend's house. You get a little wild and break a vase. Honesty is telling your friend's mother the truth and saying you are sorry.

Sometimes you do not like what is for dinner. But your dog is always hungry. Your mother asks if you ate your broccoli. Honesty is telling your mother that you fed your broccoli to the dog.

At school, you are having a hard time with an **assignment**. The person next to you is already finished. You could get the answer if you looked at her paper. Honesty is asking the teacher for help instead of looking at someone else's paper.

Many people in history have shown honesty. One of these people was Abraham Lincoln. He was known as "Honest Abe." Lincoln was the sixteenth president of the United States. He helped to end the **Civil War**.

As a young man, Abraham Lincoln owned a store. When he had to close his store, he owed people a lot of money. It took 15 years, but Lincoln paid back every cent he owed. People trusted Lincoln because he was such an honest man. Abraham Lincoln was a great example of a person who was honest.

This painting shows Abraham Lincoln giving a speech.

It is important to be honest. Being honest helps people trust you. They know you will tell the truth. How have you been honest today?

At Home

- Tell your parents when you lose your lunch money.

- Keep score correctly when you are playing a game with your brother or sister.

- Help fix something you broke.

At School

- Tell your teacher the truth even if it might get you in trouble.

- Tell your friend you will replace something you borrowed and lost.

- Let the teacher know if a classmate is doing something dangerous.

In Your Community

- Tell your neighbors if you crush their flowers during a ball game.

- Take the wallet you found in the park to the lost-and-found office.

- Return your library books on time so others can use them.

Glossary

assignment (uh-SINE-ment)
An assignment is a job that is given to someone.

Civil War (SIV-il WAR)
The Civil War was fought between the northern and southern U.S. states from 1861 to 1865.

clerk (KLERK)
A clerk is a salesperson in a store.

excuse (ek-SKYOOSS)
An excuse is a reason you give to explain why you did something wrong.

Index

To Find Out More

Books

Breathed, Berkeley. *Edwurd Fudwupper Fibbed Big.* Boston: Little, Brown, 2000.

Brenner, Martha F. *Abe Lincoln's Hat.* New York: Random House, 1994.

Cosby, Bill. *My Big Lie.* New York: Cartwheel Books, 1999.

McKissack, Patricia. *The Honest-to-Goodness Truth.* New York: Atheneum, 2000.

Web Sites

Biographies for Kids
http://www.gardenofpraise.com/leaders.htm
To learn about honesty through these stories of leaders.

Cheating
http://kidshealth.org/kid/feeling/emotion/cheating.html
To learn how to deal with cheating.

Note to Parents and Educators

Welcome to Wonder Books®! These books provide text at three different levels for beginning readers to practice and strengthen their reading skills. Additionally, the use of nonfiction text provides readers the valuable opportunity to *read to learn*, not just to learn to read.

These leveled readers allow children to choose books at their level of reading confidence and performance. Nonfiction Level One books offer beginning readers simple language, word choice, and sentence structure as well as a word list. Nonfiction Level Two books feature slightly more difficult vocabulary, longer sentences, and longer total text. In the back of each Nonfiction Level Two book are an index and a list of books and Web sites for finding out more information. Nonfiction Level Three books continue to extend word choice and length of text. In the back of each Nonfiction Level Three book are a glossary, an index, and a list of books and Web sites for further research.

State and national standards in reading and language arts emphasize using nonfiction at all levels of reading development. Wonder Books® fill the historical void in nonfiction material for primary grade readers with the additional benefit of a leveled text.

About the Author

Kathryn Kyle has taught elementary school and writes extensively for children. She lives in Minnesota.